This
book belongs

to

. . . .

THE 365 DAYS of ELOISE
MY BOOK OF HOLIDAYS

KAY THOMPSON'S ELOISE

With all-new drawings by HILARY KNIGHT

PLUS PAGES OF STICKERS

DON'T FORGET

Simon & Schuster Books for Young Readers

New York • London • Toronto • Sydney • New Delhi

for MARGUERITE from H.E.N.W. & S.

SIMON & SCHUSTER BOOKS FOR YOUNG READERS
An imprint of Simon & Schuster Children's Publishing Division
1230 Avenue of the Americas, New York, New York 10020
For information about special discounts for bulk purchases, please contact
Simon & Schuster Special Sales at 1-866-506-1949 or business@simonandschuster.com.
The Simon & Schuster Speakers Bureau can bring authors to your live event.
For more information or to book an event, contact the Simon & Schuster Speakers
Bureau at 1-866-248-3049 or visit our website at www.simonspeakers.com.
Artwork by Hilary Knight
Book design by Steve Scott
The text for this book is set in Benhard Gothic Book.
The illustrations for this book are rendered in pen and ink,
colored pencil, and watercolor.
Manufactured in the United States of America
0915 LAK
2 4 6 8 10 9 7 5 3 1
Library of Congress Cataloging-in-Publication Data
Knight, Hilary, author, illustrator.
The 365 days of Eloise : my book of holidays / by Hilary Knight ;
featuring Kay Thompson's Eloise. — First edition.
pages cm. — (Eloise)
Summary: "Adventures with Kay Thompson's Eloise for every season and holiday of the year"—Provided by publisher.
ISBN 978-1-4814-5937-2 (hardback) — ISBN 978-1-4814-5941-9 (eBook)
[1. Holidays—Fiction. 2. Seasons—Fiction.] I. Thompson, Kay, 1909–1998. Eloise. II. Title.
PZ7.K7375Aag 2015
[E]—dc23
2015014975

Hello it's me, ELOISE!

As you all know

I have a rawther exciting life

My dear NANNY gave me this

absolutely useful book

It is my monthly CALENDAR of

CELEBRATIONS and EVENTS

(of prime interest to almost everyone)

I am personally inviting

all of you to take a peek

And don't forget to look

at the very last pages to

find . . . STICKERS!

You will know exactly

what to do with them

So why don't you enter

YOUR NAME

at my private desk

Your friend,

ELOISE

January

This morning we must be very quiet
because NANNY and the top floor MAIDS
had a festive NEW YEAR'S EVE

I usually start my day with the hanging up of my new book of days
I am aware of REALITY but I do admire those who FANTASIZE so . . .
here are my NEW YEAR'S RESOLUTIONS

1. Make friends with the new PASTRY chef

2. Add Rollerblade wheels to my MARY JANES

3. Apologize to MR. SALOMONE—WEENIE bit him

4. Be more TRANQUIL—my mother's advice

5. Adopt a new HAIRDO . . . a bun could be fun

6. Remember the MAIL CHUTE is only for mail

7. Less HALL SKIBBLING . . . NANNY'S suggestion

8. Order a RAISIN soufflé for SKIPPERDEE

9. Reduce my PASTRY intake

10. . . . .

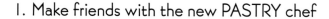

Won't you help me decide on #10 . . .
please add your personal thoughts

• NEW YEAR •

February

February 2nd
GROUNDHOG DAY

is a favorite of Weenie's
If he sees his shadow
I give him a treat!

February 12th and 22nd

Nanny and I do a double duty celebration
on PRESIDENT'S DAY in honor of
Mr. Lincoln and Mr. Washington
We made a tasty pudding for Abe and Georgie

February 14th

is perhaps one of my most favorite holidays
when I express my most intimate thoughts

· SWEET HEART ·

March

DAYLIGHT SAVINGS TIME begins

so change your clocks and timepieces and "spring ahead"

March 17th

I always celebrate ST. PATRICK'S DAY

by wearing my mother's emerald

COCKTAIL ring

It's rawther LARGE

Nanny says my mother is in Ireland collecting shamrocks

Weenie and Skipperdee helped finish
Nanny's St. Paddy's Day beverage

March comes in like a LION

· MARCH WINDS ·

April

April 1st

Every year on this day I plan a new surprise for dear old Nanny—APRIL FOOLS!

April 22nd

EARTH DAY

My bathroom makes
an ideal location for my
VEGETABLE GARDEN
Such easy cleanup

And don't forget what April showers bring

FRESH EGGS

May

Middle of May

I telephoned my mother
on MOTHER'S DAY
She was happy to hear from us

End of May

Memorial Day is for remembering

My mother
remembered to send me
this darling ensemble

· MAYTIME ·

June

Middle of June

FLAG DAY

The Plaza Hotel

always puts out my personal pennant

when I'm in residence

It is a known fact that both Nanny and Queen Elizabeth share the same birthday
Naturally we celebrate both

My mother says FATHER'S DAY
is an INVENTION

Nanny is my special comfort

· QUEEN NANNY ·

July

July 4th

For fireworks displays

we travel to the water's edge

for the best possible view

We are always impressed

For years Nanny and I have admired the needlework of Betsy Ross

· ME, BETSY ·

August

In August, every day is a holiday

VACATION TIME
When the city is sweltering
it's time to consult our collection
of travel brochures

However on particularly steamy days
we retreat to the PARK
for its refreshing breezes
Sometimes I IMAGINE
other locations

BIRD WATCH

August 21st

SENIOR CITIZENS DAY
I gave Nanny an extra hug

DREAM VACATION

September

Nanny and I begin to get into the swing of the new season

First Monday of September

LABOR DAY is of course simply the beginning of FALL FESTIVITIES

For NANNY it's the start of the FOOTBALL season

For WEENIE and SKIPPERDEE

the reason for an extended nap

I naturally turn
to the multitude
of fall fashion catalogues
to choose my winter wardrobe

Mother says CLASSIC is always best

· SCHOOL DAYS ·

October

SWEETEST DAY

Nanny and I always find ways
to celebrate this important holiday
before I become rawther scary . . .

. . . on
October 31st
HALLOWEEN

· SPOOKY ·

November

Daylight Savings Time ENDS

"Fall back"

for a complete rest

because

I am extremely busy baking

BIRTHDAY CAKES

November 1, 4, 9

for HILARY, MYSELF, and KAY

Fourth Thursday of November

THANKSGIVING is the time to gather together

NANNY says Mother has gone VEGAN. We promised to give it a try

NEW THANKS

December

December demands LISTS

I always check NANNY'S to see if anyone is missing

or to add some of my own

December 26th

BOXING DAY is when

I distribute gifts

to all my closest friends

This way to our beloved staffs

LEISURE LOUNGE

· SURPRISE ·

Oooooooooo !

We absolutely love the holidays!

Stickers!

WEENIE SAYS . . . don't look blank